ED YOUNG

Seven Blind Mice

SCHOLASTIC INC.

New York   Toronto   London   Auckland   Sydney

One day seven blind mice were surprised
to find a strange Something by their pond.
"What is it?" they cried, and they all ran home.

On Monday, Red Mouse went first to find out.

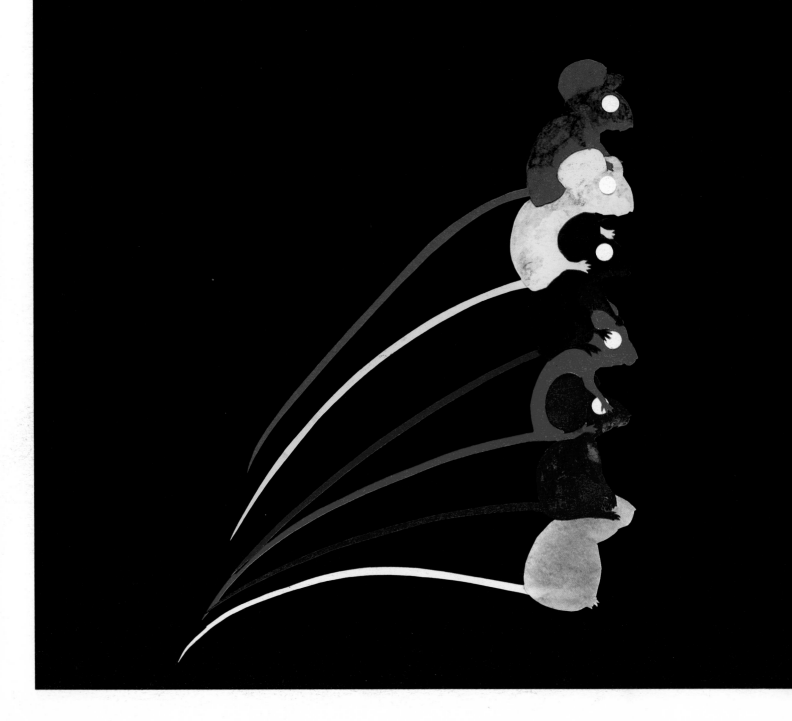

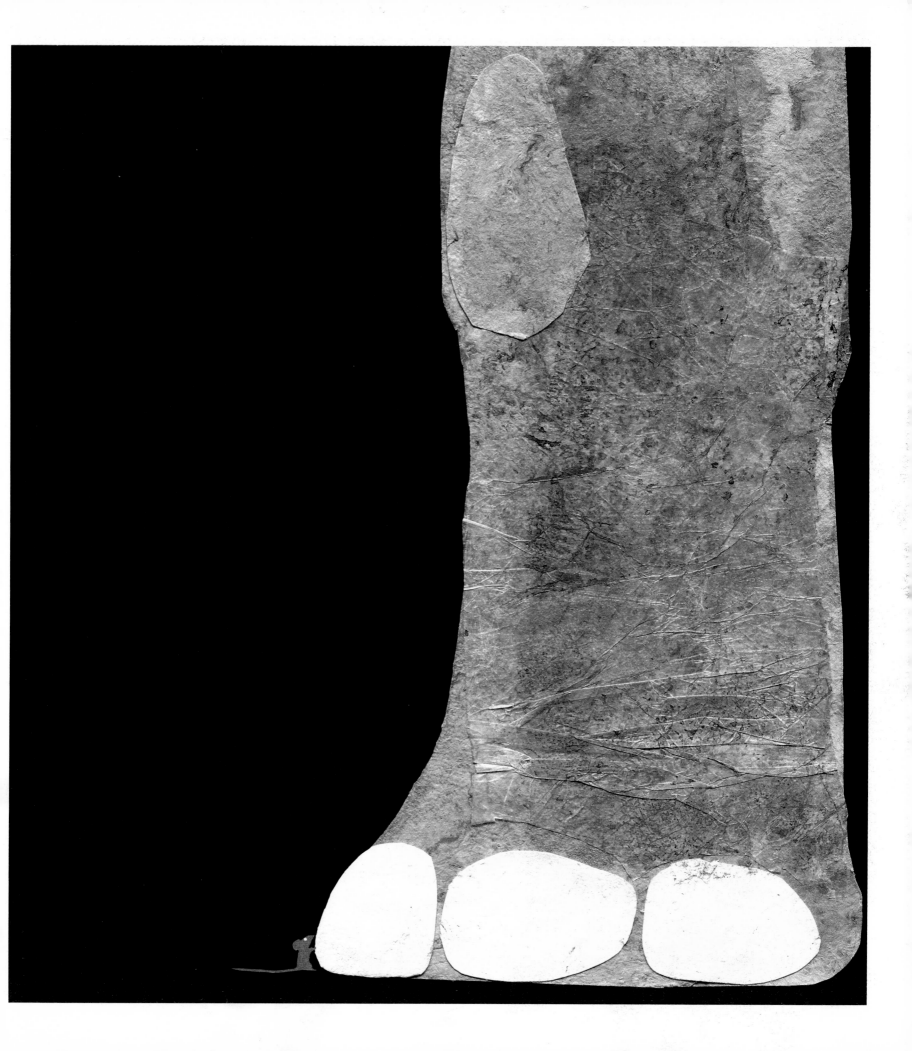

"It's a pillar," he said.
  No one believed him.

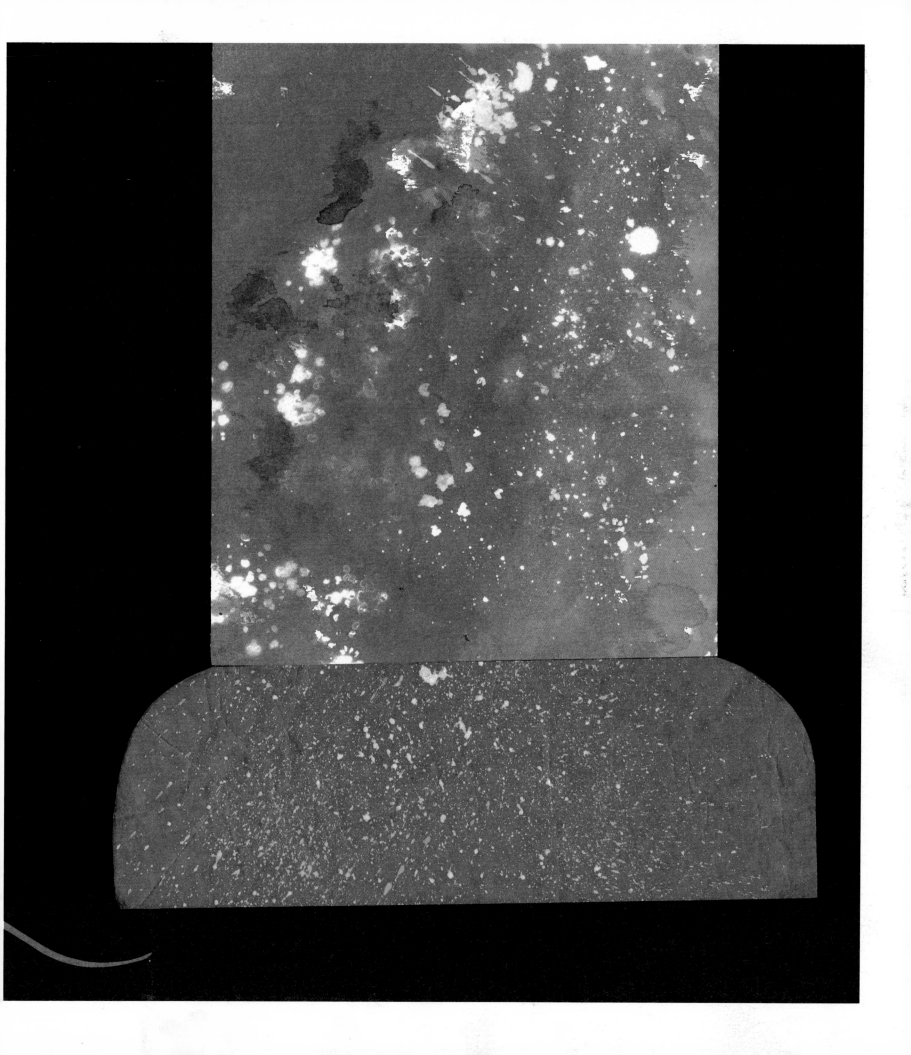

On Tuesday, Green Mouse set out.
He was the second to go.

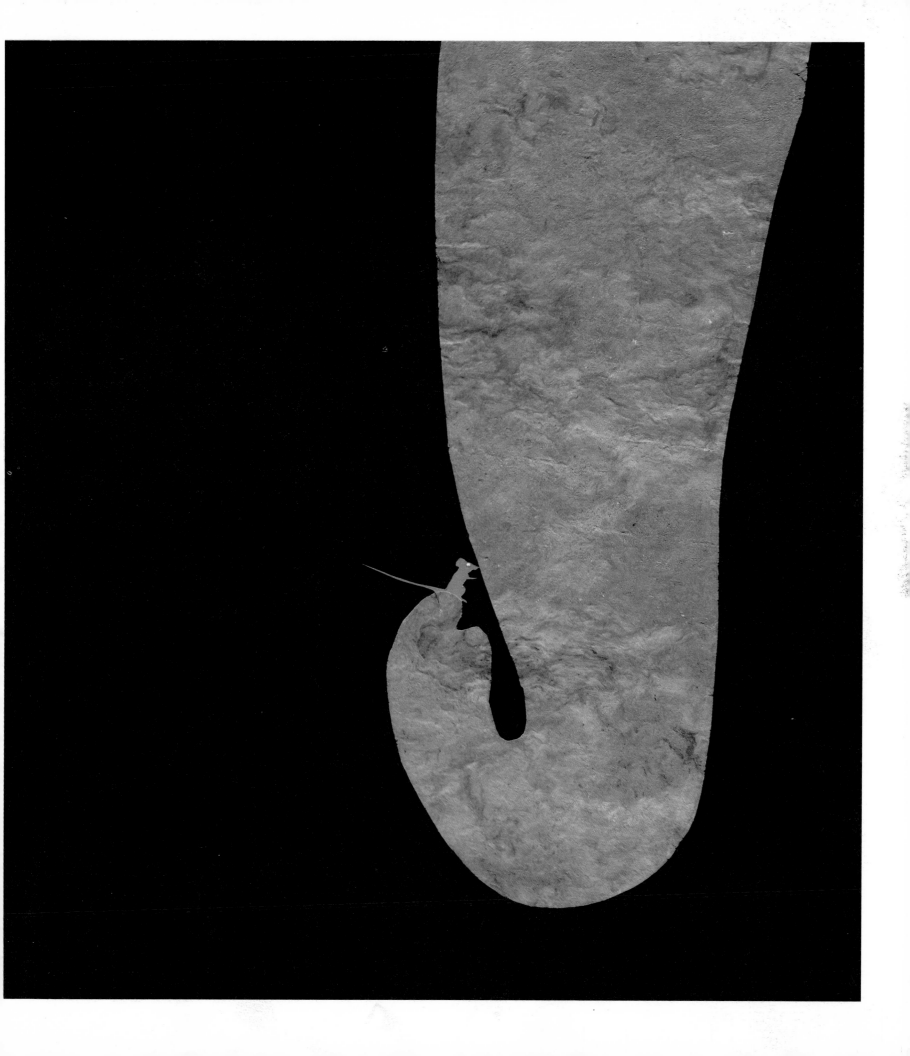

"It's a snake," he said.

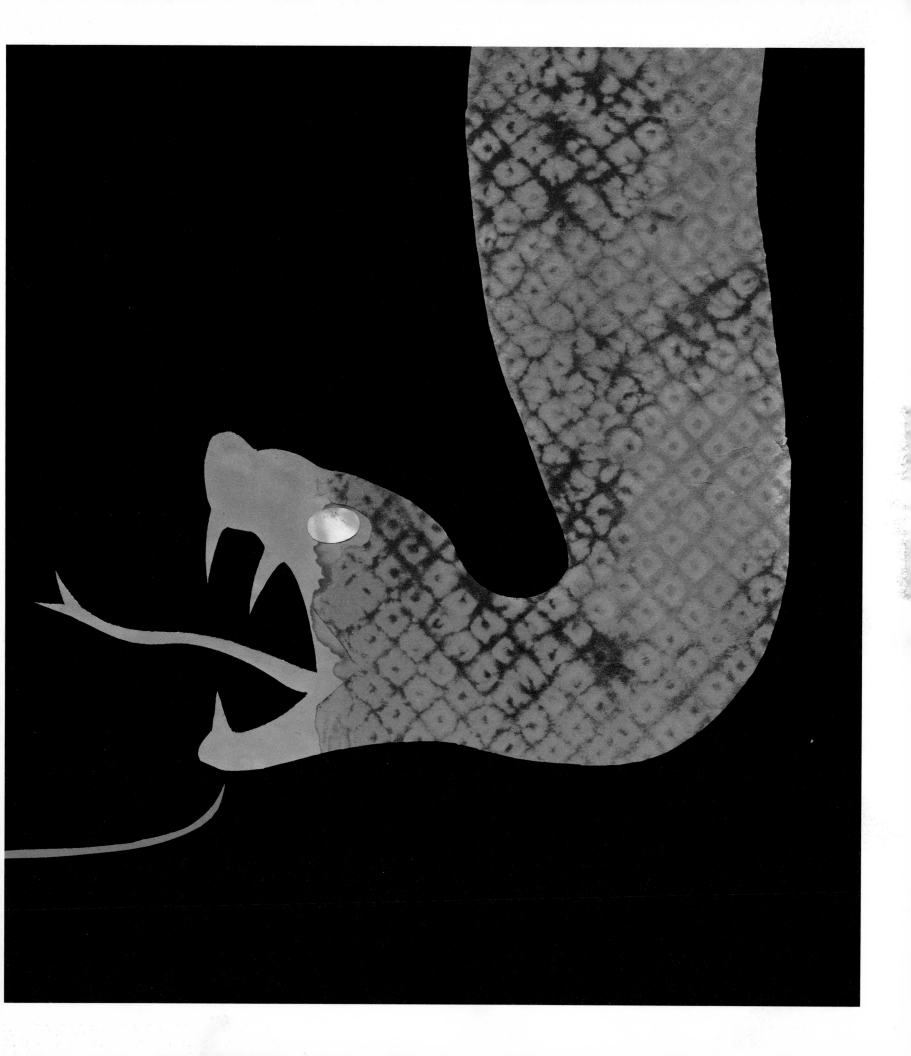

"No," said Yellow Mouse on Wednesday.

"It's a spear."
He was the third in turn.

The fourth was Purple Mouse.
He went on Thursday.

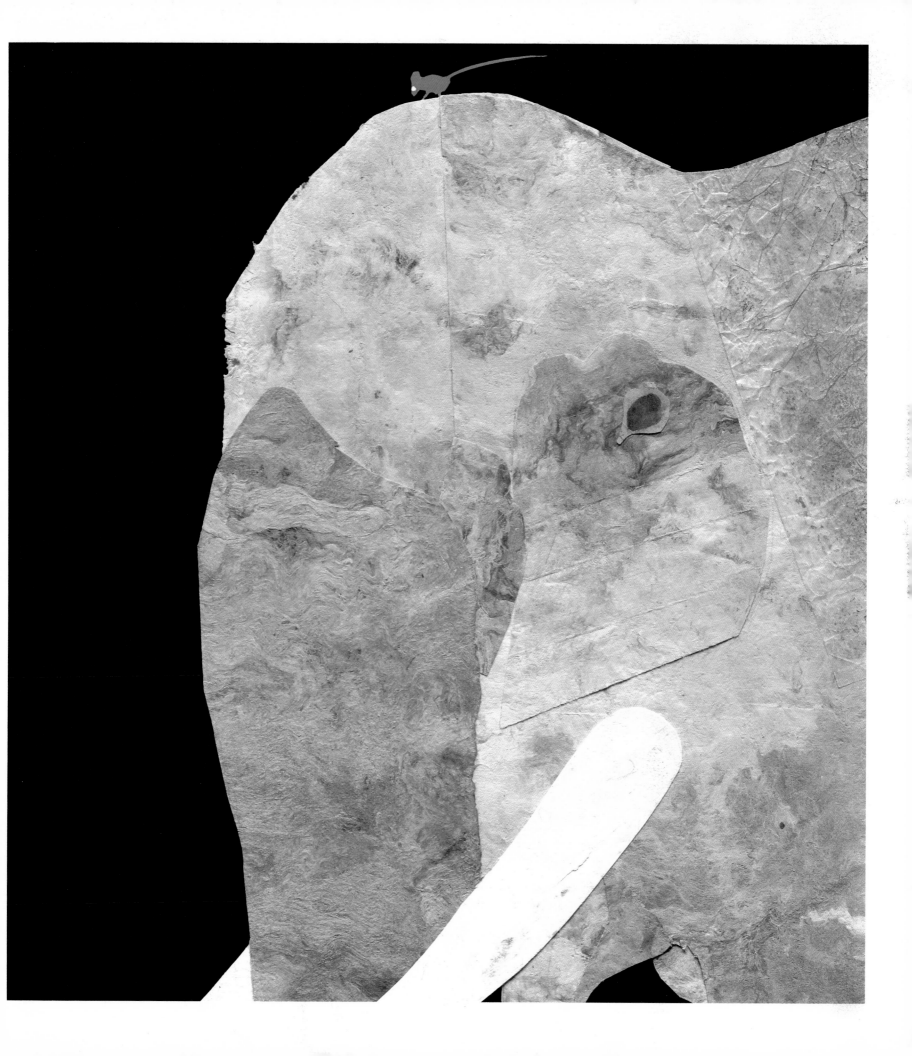

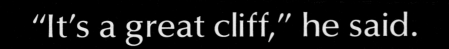

"It's a great cliff," he said.

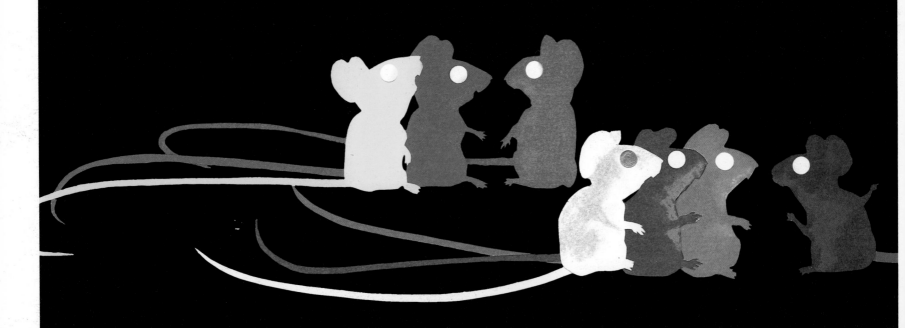

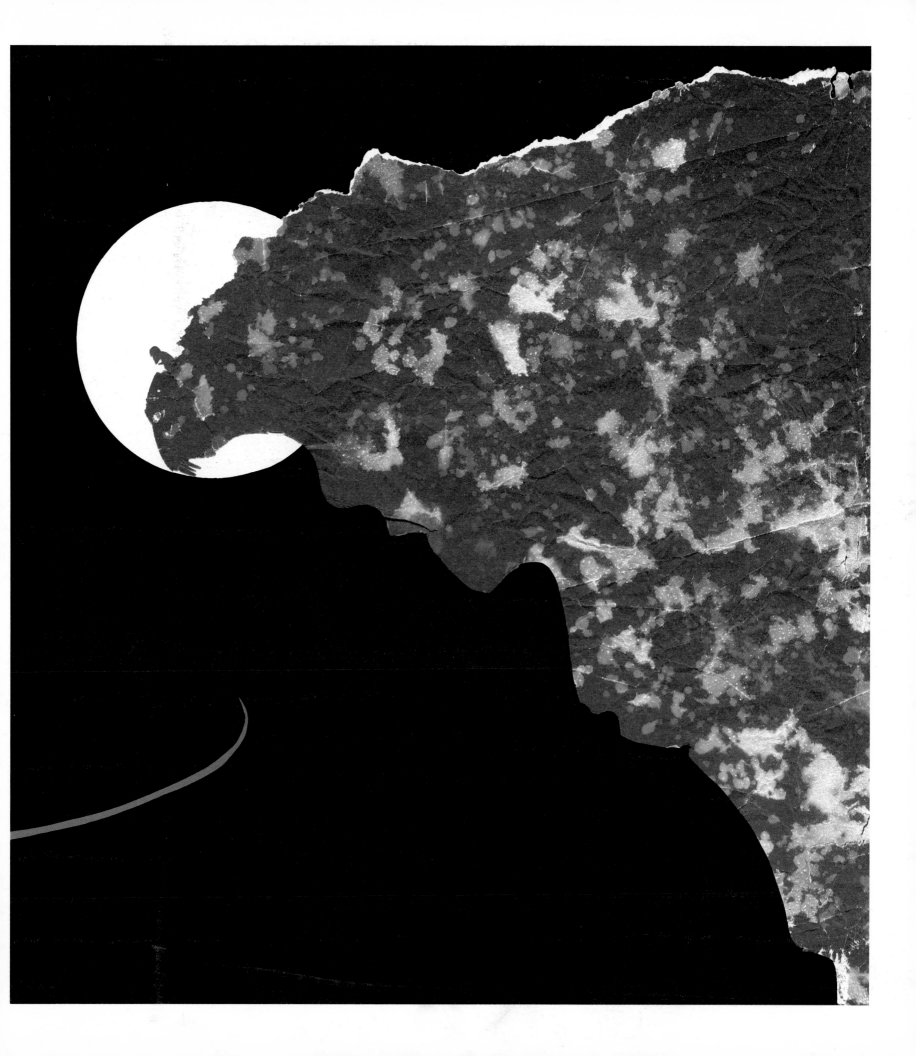

Orange Mouse went on Friday, the fifth to go.

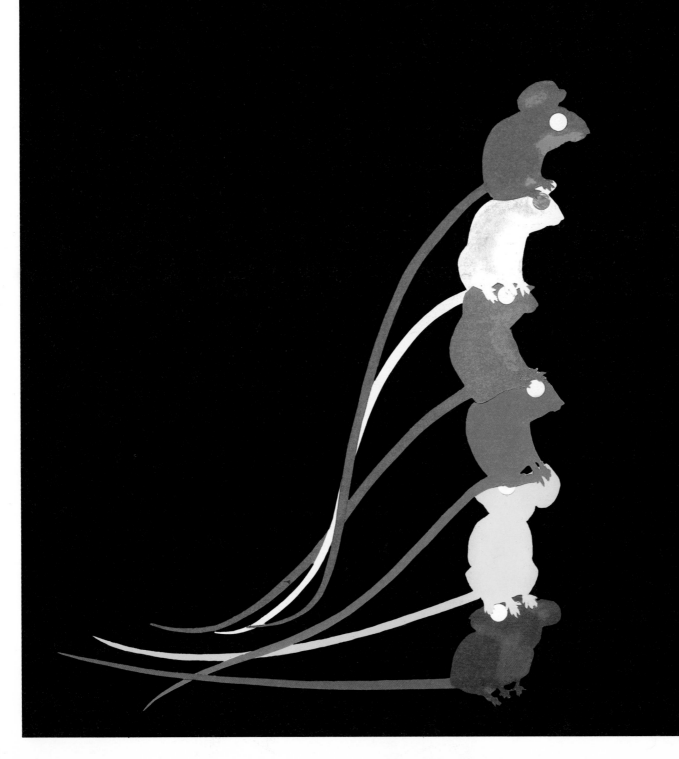

"It's a fan!" he cried. "I felt it move."

The sixth to go was Blue Mouse.

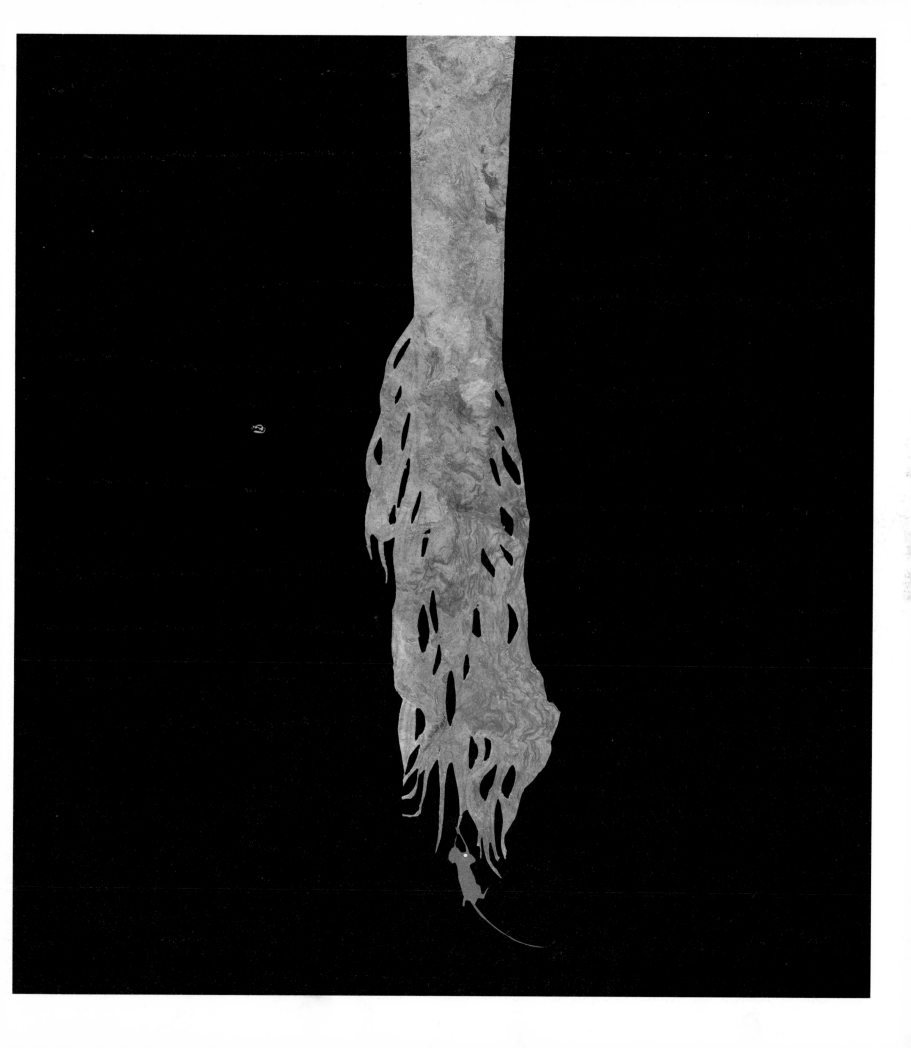

He went on Saturday and said,
"It's nothing but a rope."

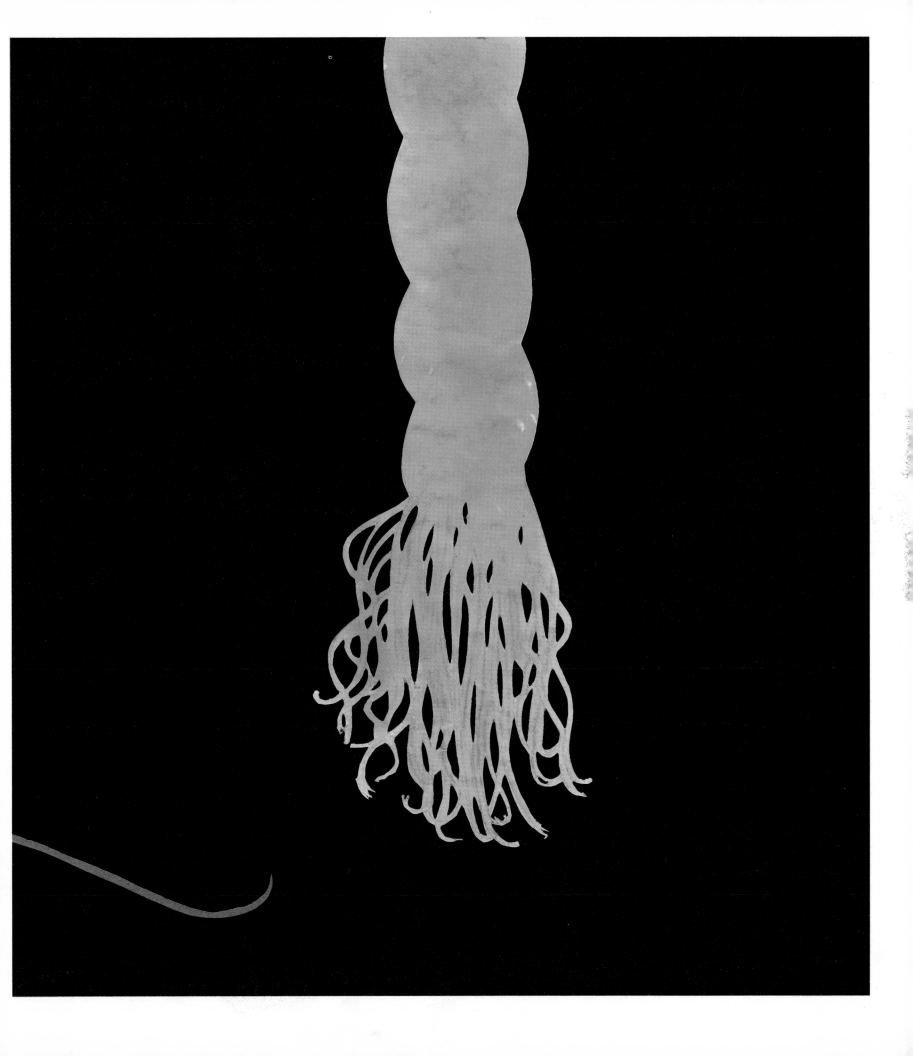

But the others didn't agree.
They began to argue.
"A snake!" "A rope!" "A fan!" "A cliff!"

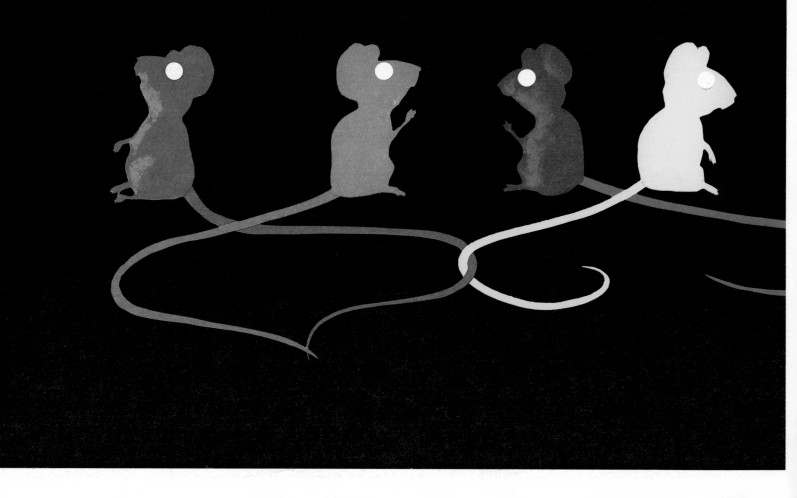

Until on Sunday, White Mouse,
the seventh mouse,
went to the pond.

When she came upon the Something, she ran up one side, and she ran down the other. She ran across the top and from end to end.

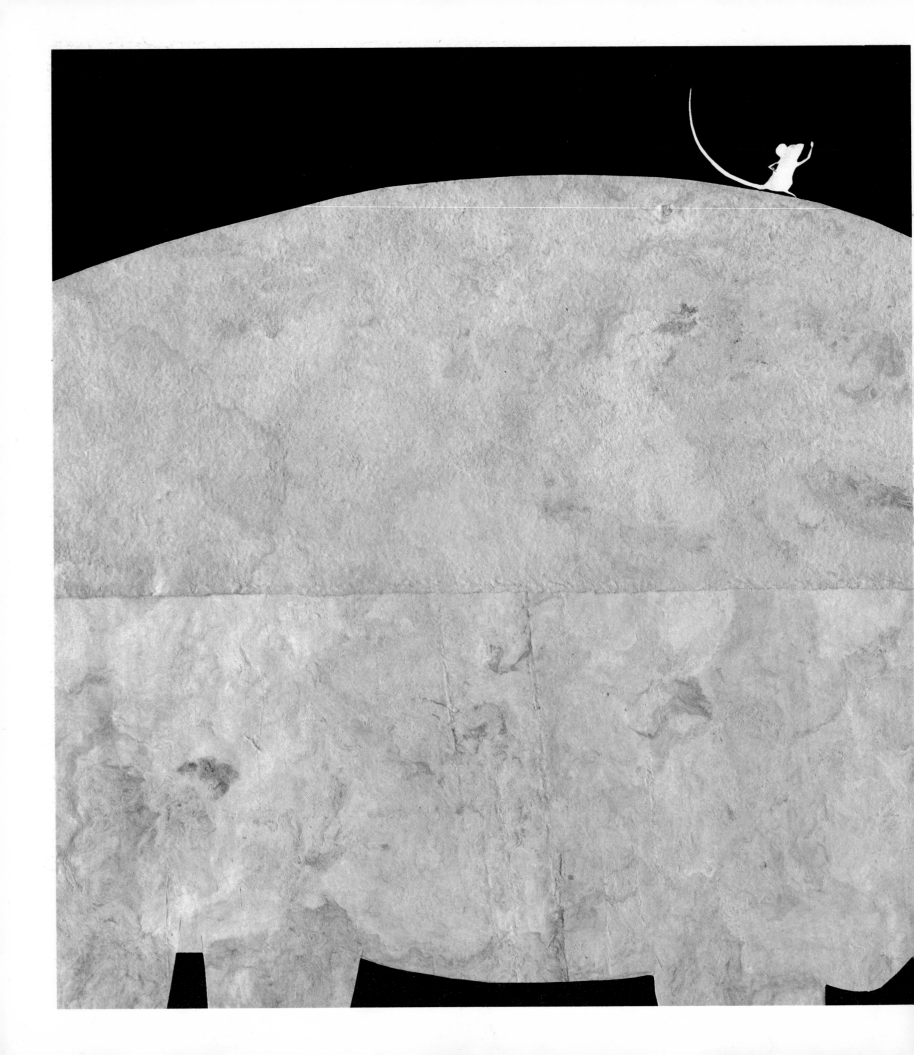

"Ah," said White Mouse. "Now, I see. The Something is
as sturdy as a pillar,
supple as a snake,
wide as a cliff,
sharp as a spear,
breezy as a fan,
stringy as a rope,
but altogether the Something is…

an elephant!"

And when the other
mice ran up one side
and down the other,
across the Something
from end to end,
they agreed.
Now they saw, too.

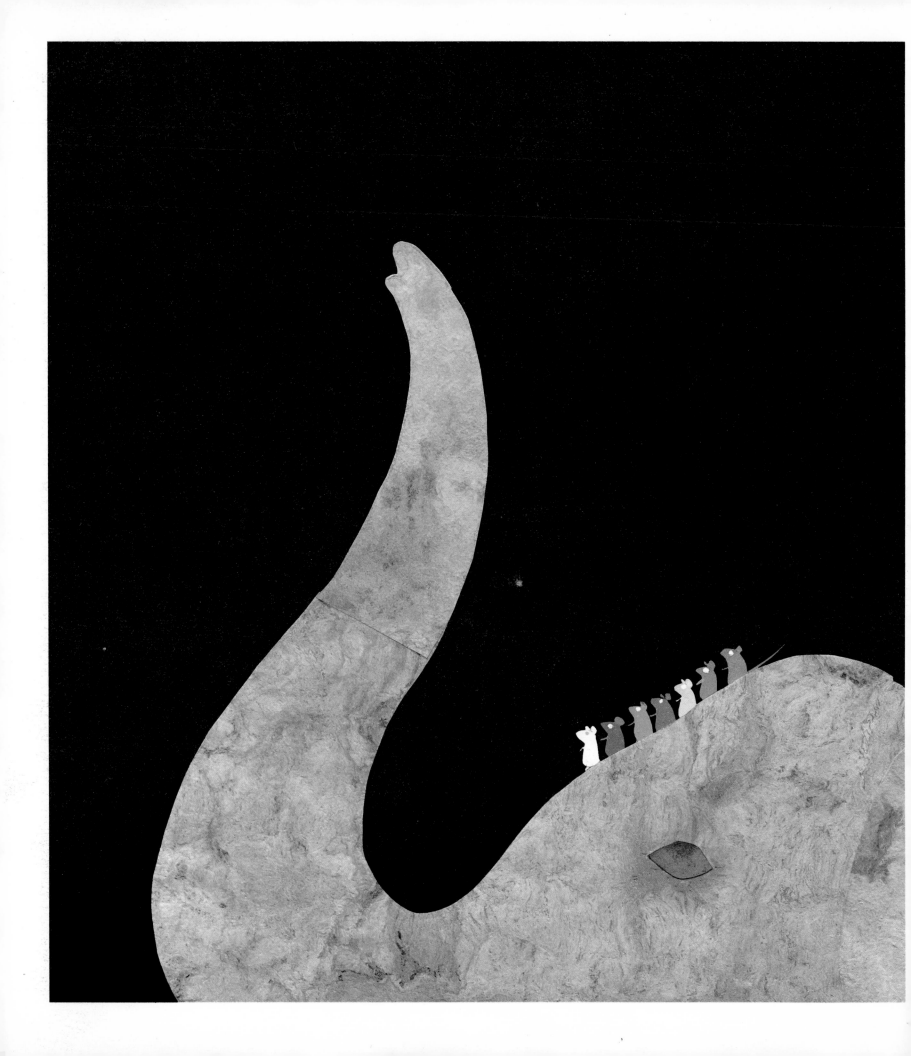

The Mouse Moral:
Knowing in part may make a fine tale,
but wisdom comes from seeing the whole.

To Wang Kwong-Mei, 艾耐哥哥
who opened my eyes to the joy
of knowledge and wisdom
in those trying years.

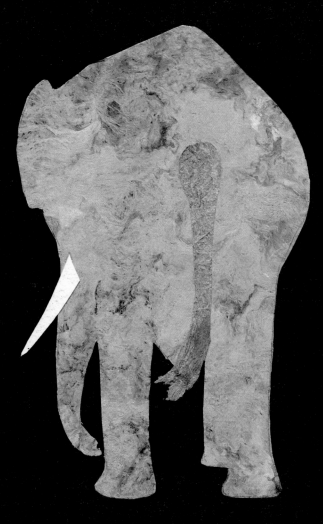

ISBN 0-590-46971-1

Copyright © 1992 by Ed Young.
All rights reserved. Published by Scholastic Inc.,
730 Broadway, New York, NY 10003, by arrangement with
Philomel Books, a division of The Putnam & Grosset Book Group.

12 11 10 9 8 7 6 5 4 3 2   3 4 5 6 7 8/9

Printed in the U.S.A.   08

First Scholastic printing, April 1993